PENGUIN BOOKS

TRIO

Three Short Stories

Jane Gardam is the author of nine ⎯⎯⎯⎯⎯⎯⎯ of stories. Her first novel won the Dav⎯⎯⎯⎯⎯⎯⎯⎯ Fiction and the Winifred Holtby Memorial Pr⎯⎯⎯⎯ twice been the winner of the Whitbread Award, most ⎯⎯ntly in 1992 for her book *Queen of the Tambourine*, and has also been shortlisted for the Booker Prize. She also won the Katherine Mansfield Award for her short stories. Her most recent book is *The Iron Coast*, her first work of non-fiction. She lives in East Kent and Swaledale.

William Trevor was educated at Trinity College, Dublin, and is a member of the Irish Academy of Letters. He is the author of many books, and has been winner of the Hawthornden Prize, the Whitbread Award (twice) and the *Yorkshire Post* Book of the Year Award. He has also been shortlisted for the *Sunday Express* Book of the Year Award and the Booker Prize. Many of his books, as well as all of his short stories, are published by Penguin, and he has also written plays for the stage, radio and television. In 1976 William Trevor received the Allied Irish Banks' Prize, and in 1977 was awarded an honorary CBE in recognition of his valuable services to literature. In 1992 he received the *Sunday Times* Award for Literary Excellence.

Rose Tremain published her first novel, *Sadler's Birthday*, in 1976. Since then, she has published five more novels and two collections of short stories, one of which won the Dylan Thomas Prize. She was named as one of twenty 'Best of Young British Novelists' in 1983. Her novel, *The Swimming Pool Season*, won the Angel Literary Award and one of her radio plays, *Temporary Shelter*, won a Giles Cooper Award. Her fifth novel, *Restoration*, was shortlisted for the Booker Prize and won the *Sunday Express* Book of the Year Award. Her most recent novel is *Sacred Country*, which won the 1993 James Tait Black Memorial Prize. Her work has been translated into six languages. She lives in Norfolk and London with the biographer Richard Holmes.

TRIO

Three Short Stories from Cheltenham

JANE GARDAM
WILLIAM TREVOR
ROSE TREMAIN

PENGUIN BOOKS

PENGUIN BOOKS

Published by the Penguin Group
Penguin Books Ltd, 27 Wrights Lane, London w8 5tz, England
Penguin Books USA Inc., 375 Hudson Street, New York, New York 10014, USA
Penguin Books Australia Ltd, Ringwood, Victoria, Australia
Penguin Books Canada Ltd, 10 Alcorn Avenue, Toronto, Ontario, Canada m4v 3b2
Penguin Books (NZ) Ltd, 182–190 Wairau Road, Auckland 10, New Zealand

Penguin Books Ltd, Registered Offices: Harmondsworth, Middlesex, England

First published 1993
1 3 5 7 9 10 8 6 4 2

Set in 11/14 pt Monotype Plantin
Typeset by Datix International Limited, Bungay, Suffolk
Printed in England by Clays Ltd, St Ives plc

Contents

Bevis   JANE GARDAM   1

A Friendship   WILLIAM TREVOR   39

The Candle Maker   ROSE TREMAIN   65

Bevis

JANE GARDAM

My cousin, Jilly Willis, a huge, leonine girl of nearly eighteen, arrived in the County Durham town where I had lived since I was born, with her mother, my Auntie Greta, and there was obviously something awful going on.

I knew it as soon as I stepped into the house from school. Something steamy. My mother stuck her head round the front room door and said, 'Tea in the kitchen. Can't come now.' This was unheard-of.

My Ma and Auntie Greta stayed shut in there together for hours. Jilly was not there. She must have been left behind at the boarding house where they'd taken rooms. I sat in the kitchen eating dried-up baked beans. I could half-hear their voices. On and on. Ma's brother, Auntie Greta's husband Uncle Alec, had died two years before. He'd been an optician and worked over towards Northumberland where he'd met and married Auntie Greta and never once came back to see us. He had been a blameless man and when we first met Auntie Greta, we were silenced. At every meeting afterwards with her, we were silenced with renewed surprise. She was a fierce raw-boned woman who never met your eyes, and always smiled. My mother could not speak of her, for she had come between her and her brother like a rough red wall.

3

Auntie Greta-Willis and Jilly stayed on in our town after the day of the secret conversation and bought a little house over the sand-hills that turned its back on everybody. They appeared to settle, and the following term Jilly started at my school. They hadn't sold their house in Northumberland because they'd left Auntie Greta's old mother in it. There seemed to be no shortage of money. Jilly was nearly six years older than I was and so at school I scarcely saw her. She was very clever. She had already been accepted on the strength of her A-level examinations by the University of Edinburgh where she was to start next year in the Science faculty, and intended to become a vet. This last year at school was to fill in time and she had decided to do an extra A-level in European History – 'To restore the balance,' my mother said. 'She won't do a year in Europe itself, like anyone else – they can't get her to shift.'

And I scarcely saw Jilly out of school either, though I think she came over to us with her mother sometimes for Sunday dinner. I sort of remember them being invited and all the rushing around to be ready for them after church. My mother and I were church-goers as Uncle Alec had been. He had been a great Christian and sung in his church choir – ethereal Uncle Alec in his nervous metal specs. I don't suppose Jilly and her mother ever went to church with him. (My mother said, 'Ah, Jilly is a pagan lady.') I don't think that Auntie Greta ever went anywhere with him. When Uncle Alec died she wrote us a note well after the funeral and my Ma wept for her brother as much as she had wept for my father. She said, 'Alec died of loneliness.'

★

'Why've they come here, Ma?'

'There's been a scandal.'

'What scandal?'

'I've sworn never to say.'

'Not even to me?'

'No. She made me promise that. Greta did. I'm very sorry.'

'Why did she?'

'Because you're only twelve.'

'Was it some sort of crime?'

'Not exactly.'

'I know. Jilly's been caught shoplifting.'

'No. Of course not.'

'People do when they're unhappy.'

'Rubbish,' said my mother. 'You didn't go shoplifting when your father died.'

When Jilly and her Ma had been living near us for about six months, the abandoned grandmother fell ill and had to be put in a Home and while all this was being arranged by Auntie Willis, Jilly came to stay with us. She seemed very big. When the three of us sat down to meals in our tiny dining-room she filled it like a doll in a box. Yet she was in no way gross or out of proportion there. All she did was make us feel under-housed. She needed marble halls. She was a foreign body.

'One day,' my mother said, 'you'll be a magnificent Roman matron and you'll wear clothes that hang from the shoulder fastened by a barbaric clip.' Jilly looked startled, rather as if she had known this herself and had been keeping it private. My mother could often say things like this. Jilly looked sharply at my Ma, and blushed. She loved it. All of a sudden she was younger and sillier and began to go floating along to the bathroom at bedtime wrapped in a counterpane tied in a shoulder-knot, tossing her mane. '*Coliseo!*' she cried and my Ma cried, '*Imperatrix!*' The house lightened. If only she could have stayed a little I think there might have been jokes. They were not quite in the air, but they were *en route*.

Her hair was bronzy and her mouth was proud. Her nose, however, was not Roman in the least but small, broad and flat like a lioness's and she had a lion's nobility about the brow. Her teeth when she smiled were small and white and square, like dice. Her eyes were not leonine but like her father's (said my Ma), large and good and grey.

When Auntie Greta came back it was to tell us that the grandmother was very comfortable in the Home now, but failing, and had need of only one thing: a last visit from Jilly.

'We could wait,' the Aunt W said. 'I don't think it's that urgent. But then, you never know. It just might be. I can't go back – it's Bank Holiday and I'm on duty.' Auntie Greta was a nurse.

My Ma said she was on duty then too. Bank Holidays were her busiest times. She was a Samaritan.

'Well, I'm certainly not letting Jilly go on her own,' I heard the Willis. 'Not by herself. Not next door again.'

'But haven't they all gone now?' said Ma. 'There are new people next door now.'

'I'm not having her anywhere near. Not by herself. Not next door again even if it's empty.'

6

'Who's moved in there?'

'I've no idea and I don't want to know.'

'Couldn't she stay with the Chalmers? They were nice people. They were good friends to Alec. Before . . .'

'I'm afraid I never took to them at all.'

I'd been hanging about listening and they found themselves staring at me. Then they started coughing and pouring themselves more tea and behaving as though they'd been saying nothing at all. The Willis gave a sly look at her big bold palms. Ma said, 'I suppose you wouldn't like to go away for a weekend with Jilly, hinny? Back to her old home to see her gran in hospital? Stop her feeling homesick?'

'There'd be nobody else in the house,' said the Willis. 'You could do what you wanted, with Granny in The Gables. You could have plates on your knees and we haven't got rid of the telly yet. I'd maybe stand you a café tea.'

I went on painting my nails. I had my own friends and my own plans for Bank Holiday and I didn't believe that Jilly could still be homesick when I thought of the counterpane.

'Is that my nail varnish?' asked Ma.

'I'd soon put a stop to that,' said the Willis. 'I'd have given Jilly what-for for nail muck at thirteen.' She turned her empty teacup into the saucer to read the tea-leaves. You could see what her mouth would be like in old age. A draw-string purse tight shut. Everything was in-growing with Greta. Her chest was concave below her great shoulders. I wondered if her breasts grew inwards too.

'I'm sure she'll go,' said Ma, 'won't you, hinny? Because of Jilly's grandma – won't you?'

'Would Jilly want me?'

'She's easy,' said the Willis. 'There's one thing I'd ask, though. You'd have to promise to keep near her. Keep close.'

'Oh, I'd be fine,' I said. 'I've been youth-hostelling by myself. I've been on a French exchange.' (I'd hardly seen my French exchange as it happened, though they didn't know it. I'd wandered all over Paris alone while Dominique sat looking *soignée* in bars, chain-smoking and behaving twenty-five. Her parents fortunately had made no inquiries about our views on the statues in the Louvre and my mother had not yet been made aware of the non-improvement in my French. That was to come.)

'No,' said the W. 'What I mean is, that you mustn't let Jilly go off alone. You mustn't leave her for a minute. See?' She was glaring at me like black ice.

'Is something the matter with Jilly?'

'She's not very well,' said Ma. 'Out of kilter. Out of true.'

'Teen-age,' said the W and took out her handkerchief. She wiped her hands and dried off the corners of her mouth.

'Whatever did happen?' I asked when she'd gone. 'You'll have to tell me. It's not fair on me if you don't. Or safe. I shan't know the danger signals.'

'Oh, duck,' said Ma, 'oh my hinny. I promised but I'll –'

'What?'

8

'I'll give you a –'.

'Clue?'

'No. Not a clue. I promised. I'll give you a whatsit? Example. Metaphor. Little story. Something I once saw and I've never forgotten.'

'Oh, Lord.'

'Listen. I was on the top of a tram once, long ago. The tram had stopped in the middle of the road, as they did – as they do. It was when I was a student abroad somewhere. Standing on the pavement waiting for someone was a man. Reading a newspaper. He was old. Well, he seemed old to me. He may have been fifty or he may have been sixty – there's no difference when you're eighteen. The fact of him though was that he was most marvellously good-looking. I don't mean Byronic. Don Juanish. Flashy foreigner. He could have been from anywhere in the Western world. But he was a truly handsome man. I can still see him. "Beautiful" sounds soft, but, well – he was beautiful. There. I remember thinking, like a god. One of the old gods.

'Well, off the bus gets this girl and hinny, she was plain! Not fascinatingly ugly or quaint or arresting – just plain. Very very ordinary, with thick glasses and lank hair and fat little bottle legs. She called out to the man and he looked up and dropped the newspaper on the pavement and smiled and held out his arms and she ran in to them.'

'It was her father.'

'It was not her father.'

'How did you know?'

'I knew. It was huge, romantic love.'

'Oh, wow.'

'No. Not oh wow. Don't play tired of life at thirteen. It was love. They stood clasped together with people going round them as if they were a sculpture. Oblivious. After the tram started and swung round to the side at the end of the road I could still see them, still clasped together. And this was Italy. Maybe Holland. Not London. You'll know what that means one day.'

'So then?'

'So then, nothing. It just happened. So think.'

'Think what?'

'Think that there are some queer goings-on.'

I asked, 'Can we have the telly on now?' and Ma said, 'Oh, hin. I'm sorry. You're just a bairn. I've been asking a lot.'

'You mean, making me go away with Jilly?'

'Yes,' she said. 'Maybe that, too.'

We went first to the Home and it smelled of mince. I said I'd wait for Jilly in the hall and she said, 'It's all right. I don't mind you coming in with me to see her, you know. It might even be better.'

'It's you she wants to see. I'd just fuddle her up.'

'Suit yourself,' she said. 'She won't exactly wave the flags when I walk in. That's just Mamma. She never liked me and she hated Dad. Pass that mag over.'

'Why can't you go on up now?'

'They said to wait. They're turning her. She's had a stroke. Didn't you know? You can come in with me. Are you frightened?'

'Why should I? She's not mine. Of course I'm not frightened.'

'Can you come now, dearie?' A fat lady had appeared

round a cardboard wall that was pressed up against the banister of a coiled mahogany staircase that had once known crinolines. Hair sprouted about round her nurse's cap, pinned on crooked with hairslides. Whiskers stuck out of her chin and she was smoking. She looked more like an inmate than a nurse, but that's England now, as Ma would say.

'I'll be outside,' I said.

'You can bring your friend. She won't mind.'

I fled and kicked the gravel outside until Jilly reappeared, looking glassy. She hadn't been gone ten minutes. She said, 'We may as well walk on then, from here.'

We passed a pub called The Pit Laddie, and then a ramshackle bus passed us full of tired Indians. I said, 'What a lot of Indians all together,' and Jilly said, 'They're miners, fool. It's dirt. Haven't you been anywhere?'

We walked by the grand big clock-works of the coal face and up a steep cobbled street where women with folded arms leaned against door-frames scratching above their elbows. They looked golden Jilly up and down, saying nothing.

'Gran came from round this way,' she said.

'Did she know who you were?'

'She just looked. She rolled her eyes about.'

'Did you talk to her?'

'Listen – shut up. I'll tell you one day when you're older. It's not important anyway.'

'You don't care about anybody, Jilly, do you? You don't care about a single human being.'

'Oh, no,' she said. 'Oh, most absolutely no. Miss Angel.'

★

We left the hilly strip streets and reached the ridge of the town above, where there was a new spread of small red houses and shops with the new-fangled metal window-frames. We came to other new houses built in groups and called after places in the Lake District: Derwent Crescent, Windermere Walk, Esthwaite Close. They were semi-dets, two and two, divided down the middle. The longer we walked the more money had been spent on lawn-mowers, azaleas, plastic ponds, gnarled stumps of Disneyesque plastic trees. Gnomes fished. The last two houses were the finest, a low box hedge separating the gardens. On one side of it the grass was a foot high and full of weeds, on the other shorn and edged with metal strip. On the well-kept lawn a man crouched, clipping precisely up to the middle of the hedge in a half knees-bend. Intently. Awkwardly. Snip, snip. Jilly wheeled towards the door of the scruffy house and opened the gate, which gave a cry. The man most carefully did not look at us but continued expertly snipping, then rose and went indoors.

Jilly produced a key and entered her old home which lay in semi-darkness and had an airless, old person's smell. She felt across a sofa and shut her eyes.

'What do we do now?' I asked after a bit. 'Jilly?'

'Suit yourself.'

Looking about, I saw nothing that suited at all. The furniture of the whole house seemed to have been gathered into the room. A bed stuck out from a wall between a sideboard and a wardrobe. On a gummy, dusty dining-table stood pots of marmalade, packets of corn-flakes and old library books. Burned bread-and-milk stood black in a saucepan on the eau-de-Nil tiles of the lounge fireplace. Copper things on leather straps, ornamental bronze shovels, warming-pans and a brass lady who wagged a bell-clapper under her skirts were reminders of more confident times. Uncle Alec's degree in Optometry hung framed on a wall near a flight of flapping china ducks. There was a knock on the front door.

'Mr Bainbridge just saw you as he was attending to the party hedge,' said the next door Mrs. 'We just wondered if there was any news of Granny.'

'Oh,' I said, 'she's not mine. She's Jilly's.' I turned, but Jilly made signals with her arms, not opening her eyes.

'Anything we can do,' said Mrs Bainbridge. 'Anything.' She tried not to peer. 'We'd be glad. We've been so worried. We're only newcomers ourselves and we didn't want to impose. And we couldn't make her daughter hear when we rang the bell last week when she came to take her off. Granny got in a terrible state, you know. We notified some mutual acquaintances, the Chalmers, and they were the ones sent out the alert to the daughter – that would be,' (peering) 'your mother?'

Jilly was continuing to signal. 'Get rid of her. Close the door.'

'Of course, it's the old next-door neighbours I blame,' said the woman. 'The people before us. They took no concern for her at all, no matter him being a Latin teacher at the Comp. Useless stuff. And very standoffish to all round about. Too good for this neighbourhood. Very well-to-do, though how I can't think on teacher's pay. Well, *she* had money. And a nice price they got out of us for the house and never a word about painted-over rotten window-sills. Hello, dear.' Jilly had materialized beside me. 'Just the two of you here alone? Well, that does seem a shame on your Bank Holiday.'

'We've been to The Gables to see my grandmother.'

'Well, I'm very glad. I *am* glad. I've just been saying to your sister –'

'Cousin.'

'Sorry, dear, cousin. I've just been saying . . . Could I just step inside? Oh, dear – that pan. And all those grease marks round the chair. That'll bring mice. I was saying, I blame the neighbours before. The people before us. They could have found out who to contact. We knew nobody crescent-wise and they'd been here for years. Just as you had, dear. Born here, weren't you? Very cold people you had next door. Southerners, I dare say, and always away foreign. Would you both like a bit of something?'

'No thanks,' I said. 'We've been told to go to the Chalmers.'

'Actually, yes. We would,' said Jilly. 'Thanks, we would.'

'Half an hour, then? Give me time to make things nice.'

'I don't want to go,' I said. 'Whyever did you say we'd go? We could have had chips.'

'Or gone to the Charming Chalmers like Mummy said, Little Lambkin.'

'No – I don't want to go to the Chalmers.' (I was shy with the Chalmers. They sent big presents at Christmas and I never could get my thank-you letters to sound grateful enough. They were gods in the shadows.) 'I just don't want to go in next door. They're busy bodies. And if they'd really cared about your Gran they wouldn't have let her eat out of pans.'

'You didn't know my Gran,' said Jilly. 'No,' she said, 'we'll go. We may as well. There'll be hot water and they might let us have a bath. Everything's switched off here.'

'Your mother isn't a very good organizer, is she?'

'Well, she's not all over you all the time and she's kept her figure.'

Cold at heart, for I was a retarded thirteen and still believed that all other girls were jealous of me because my mother was so incomparably better than theirs – I spoke not one word as I followed Jilly up the tidy side of the hedge towards Mr Bainbridge who was holding open his front door and looking down at the path in order not to see Jilly's legs. Inside the door, what should have been the mirror-image of Jilly's house was frighteningly different. A forest of new chairs in Jacobean print covers stood on high-glaze parquet and all was open-plan behind slatted rainbow blinds.

'We had to do a great deal of work here,' said Mrs Bainbridge, 'a lot of knocking through. The last people – well, it hadn't been changed since the war. Finger-plates above the doorknobs with Greek ladies carrying jars and irises and daffodils in plaster-work round the lounge fireplace. And little bits of stained glass. It was a scream.'

'We're told it was an intellectual family,' said Mr Bainbridge, *Reader's Digest* open by his plate. He seemed troubled by something and put his serviette to his face and smelled it.

'It's my scent,' said Jilly, not looking at him.

'The man before – the teacher – he'd had foreign education and a varsity degree. Oh, yes, it's a good neighbourhood,' said Mr Bainbridge. 'I wonder if your mother has had any thoughts yet – could you ask her? – about the selling of the house, strokes being what they are. Naturally it affects us. Price-wise the right people will be important in the crescent. One has to take an interest.'

'Could I go upstairs?'

They looked surprised. Jilly was two bites into her fish pie.

Mrs B said, 'Of course, dear. First on the left.'

'I know.'

She disappeared up the spiral staircase for what seemed hours. The Bainbridges were uneasy. They talked brightly on but appeared to be listening. I wondered what they'd heard about Jilly and again I had the random thought about stealing. Why did I always come back to the thought of Jilly as a taker? A danger? A foreigner among us all?

She was back, looming above us over the white wrought iron. She looked flushed. 'Mr Bainbridge,' she said, 'could I ask you for something very special? A very special favour? A loan?'

He turned pink through his light moustache. 'Of course, my d –'

'Have you a bike? Could we borrow a bike for tomorrow? We don't have to be home before evening and we can't spend the whole day sitting with Gran.'

There was a fractional hesitation before Mr Bain-bridge said, 'Yes,' and Mrs Bainbridge said, 'I'm afraid Mr Bainbridge only has his racing bikes. He's been a professional, you know. Connected with the Luton Twelve.'

'We'd take great care of it.'

'Yes. Yes, of course,' said Mr Bainbridge.

After supper he brought ticking through the house a flimsy, finely drawn grasshopper with slim crossbar and a saddle like a whippet.

'Twenty-seven ounces,' he said. 'Hero of the Luton Twelve.'

'*And* the Bedford Four,' said Mrs Bainbridge.

Mr Bainbridge was stroking the saddle and looking at Jilly's legs, starting low, gliding upwards. 'Do you think you can manage it?'

'Oh, it's not for me, it's for her,' Jilly said, looking straight at him and smiling. 'Mine's still in Gran's shed. Don't worry, my cousin's a terrific rider.'

'But I've never –'

'You are very kind' – she looked at him again – 'we'll take the greatest care of it.'

'Would you like a practice run?' asked Mr B as we left, looking at my legs quite differently, finding them unreassuring.

'Oh, she's terribly good,' said Jilly.

In the gran's house I said, 'You're awful, Jilly. You're deceitful. You're mad, too. I can't ride a bike like that.'

'We'll have a dummy run first thing tomorrow. You'll be OK.'

'*You* can ride it.'

'I can't ride it. I'm far too heavy. I can just cope with my own and it's like a sofa. We'll get up early. We'll go to bed now.'

In the morning we wheeled the two bikes respectfully away from Wast Water Crescent and down the cobbled hill to The Gables.

'You keep going round the gravel till I'm out,' she said, and when she came back I was tottering in zigzags, heading for easy jumping-off places, but making a little progress.

'How is she?'

'She's a lot better. They've been feeding her gravy.'

'*Gravy?*'

'She likes gravy. Don't look like that. She always liked it. She slurped it up with a spoon. She used to fill up her Yorkshire puddings with it, like a pond, and it used to spill out all over her great bits of beef. She liked her beef leathery like tongues in shoes. She used to slap her lips, slap, slap. She dribbled. She always dribbled. Her mouth perpetually watered. She was always foul.'

'Don't look so saint-like,' she said. 'There are horrible people, and I hate her.'

We pushed the bikes up the cobblestone slopes of little houses and soon came out to open country with high blue hills along the horizon, and a great sky. Clouds rolled over it like tumbleweed in Westerns.

'She used to beat me.'

'*What?*'

'My gran. She called it "leathering". She used to leather me with a belt. Grow up.'

'But your *mother* was there!'

'She'd been leathered by her too. Sometimes they both leathered me together. What's the matter? D'you want me to help you up on the bike? Why've you gone white?'

'But your *mother!* She was married to Uncle Alec. My mother's own brother.'

'Oh, Dad used to turn white too. He used to go and sit in the shed while it was going on. I used to scream. It was when I was little.'

'Shut up, shut up, shut up.'

'It's all right. Dad's dead. He was weak. *Il souffre* but *il est mort*. Gran soon will be, thank God. I don't give a toss for her. Or my mother.'

'But Jilly, there's always a reason for wickedness. *Jilly!*'

She had leaped on the lumbering bike and begun to push the pedals down, one-two, with her strong legs until she was away over the hill. After an unpromising start and a fall or two on the lonely road I clenched my teeth and got the hang of it. Soon I was understanding the gears.

I came up alongside Jilly and flew past her. I stopped, one foot on a boulder, balancing with my hand against the stone wall that accompanied us over the moor like a snake, westward towards the Irish Sea.

'Wherever are we going, Jilly?'

She was heaving her bike up the hill towards me, one leg pressing down, then the other, head turning left and then right. She was like a solemn giant, slowly dancing.

'We're going to his new house. I'm going to see him again.'

'Whose house?'

'Use your empty head. Our old neighbours.'

'D'you know the address?'

'Yes. He told me it. Before we left he managed to get a note to me, God knows how, but he's brilliant. We both knew – we'd always known – I'd have to go the minute they found out. It was a matter of time. We knew that. One of us would have to move. I'd pretty well finished at the Comp. It was his school too, but – well, we knew of course it'd have to be me.'

'Jilly – what happened?'

'Do you honestly not know?'

And I did know, of course. In the cradle, at the breast, probably in the womb we know. When they announce what they call the facts of life they are never really a surprise.

'No, I don't,' I shouted as she pedalled on past me and away towards the purple banked-up clouds ahead.

'How far is it, Jilly? How far?'

I caught her up and began to weave about around her and then diagonally in front of her, across and across the road.

'Jilly? Jilly, can we stop and have the chocolate? Jilly?'

On she went, and passed me.

'Not far now,' she called as the first big drops fell and the wind began. 'Bloody cold,' she called.

'Where are we *going*? There aren't any houses up here. It's mad. I'm going back.'

'Fine. Go.'

'I promised not to leave you.'

'In case what? Did they say why? In case I went off with him? In case I got kidnapped by him?'

'I don't know what you're talking about, Jilly. Honestly. I don't.'

The rain had become cold and soaking by the time we had climbed the next long hill, Jilly plugging up it slower and slower but never giving up, never getting off to walk. I'd been pushing my bike for some time already. It was so light that I had to walk beside it to hold it down. It was trying to blow away over the wall into the heather.

To the north of our walled road I saw a blacker, higher, more organic-looking ridge squirming out of sight. It looked as old as the rock.

'Whatever is it, Jilly?'

'Roman Wall. We're nearly there.'

'Roman this, Roman that. *Jilly!*' I remembered Mother going on about Jilly belonging to another country. I had an exhausted, frightened knowledge that she was pedalling me away to it, and out of time – I didn't know whether forward or backward. But I did know that where she was going wasn't for me.

She seemed to be almost flying ahead now and the rain flung itself on the shiny lilac road and the wind struck me in the face. There was a great space of empty moor all round, not a building, not a signpost.

'*Jilly!*'

I saw her ahead, turning left, south, down a dirt track, out of sight, and I followed her, bumping over stones into a dip, out of a dip, then as we climbed again one behind the other we were all at once beside a long metal field-gate standing wide open. Just inside and to the right was a tin-roofed Dutch barn and across what once had been an old Northumbrian farmyard but now had flowers planted in its horse-trough was a spruced-up farmhouse painted glittering white. Two stables now fitted with metal up-and-over garage doors stood near by. An ornamental wagon wheel, also painted white, was arranged beside a smartened-up old pump and there was the start of a rockery – very sparse – on what had been a midden. No sign of an animal; not a cat, not a chicken, and not one weed in the shining cobbles. I saw all this only after we had both collapsed inside the open-sided barn and could look out at it through rain that fell like silver arrows. Jilly let her bike drop and went round a corner, to sit on a hay block, knees apart, hands clasped, bowing her wet head. Her hair was plastered against her skull, dark and dripping, as I suppose was mine.

'Jilly?'

I burrowed about, pulling at the hay, trying to get some loose to put it round me like bedclothes. Before us was a great view of sky and fell, the cocky, ravished farmhouse behind. Through the rain, towards the road I saw some flashes of light, like swords, far away. Then the sky cleared, the flashes vanished and the sun came out with ice-cold raindrops still striking down from clouds blown away. Like light from dead stars, the view, sopped with rain dazzled, and sunlight caught a distant bracelet of Roman Wall, then left it.

'They must have had days like this,' I said.

'Who must?'

'The Romans.'

She said nothing.

I said, 'They must have got ever so depressed. So cold. So far from Italy and nobody talking Latin.'

'They'd been here long enough,' she said. 'They'd probably forgotten Latin. They'd have talked pidgin English – chop-chop and doolally and that. It was like home here. Well, all Europe was home then. Anyway, they were soldiers, weren't they? They were used to it. It's the girls back home you've to be sorry for – left behind with the wimps. They were the ones to be depressed.'

It was nice she was thinking of all this instead of –

'Jilly,' I said, 'let's go back. This place is empty. They're all away. They'll be away for Bank Holiday.'

'Yes.' Her voice was dead.

After a while she said, 'They'll be at the boat.'

'Boat?'

'They've a boat. They have everything. Been everywhere. He has everything. Everything in the world that life can give.'

'He hasn't got you, Jilly. I bet he misses you.'

She leaned over to her bike and burrowed in the saddle-bag and brought out a notebook and a pencil and scribbled something.

'Jilly. Jilly – what's his name?'

'Bevis.'

'*Bevis*.'

'Yes,' she said, 'Bevis. Why not?'

'I don't know. It's a bit –'

'It's Latinate,' she said. Solemnly.

Our eyes met across the hay. And held. '*Bevis!*'

Held unblinking.

I had the extraordinary notion that the gods were assembled and were on my side. I might save Jilly now.

'It's a family name,' she said with hauteur.

I said, 'Coo-er!'

Her lips and nose for a lovely instant twitched. But then – 'And what, may I ask, does that mean, Po-face?'

'Well, isn't it – a bit sort of comic?'

'*Comic?*' Oh, very proud. Swallowing. Tossing back the lion's drying mane. Glaring down the lion's flat nose.

'Well, you know. It sounds like some sort of bread.'

'*Bread?*'

'Or some sort of beverage. A sort of wheatgerm drink.'

'*Beverage!*'

Our eyes held steady and then hers flickered and her mouth trembled and I thought, I've done it. She'll laugh.

But no.

She turned her head and sank sideways in the hay and the wind kicked the tin roof of the barn about and clattered it like a thunder-sheet. With plumes of water at its wheels a long car with a boat behind it on a trolley came rollicking down the track from the moor and swept through the farm gate. A great many people shot out of the car and disappeared into the house.

Jilly did not stir.

'Jilly, they're back. The family's back.'

Now down the lane came the flashes I had seen before, far off, a group of cyclists in shiny black-beetle capes, peaked caps and bikes as ritzy as mine. In the tracks of the car they swooped into the yard and over to the barn and dismounted all around us, wet through. Ignoring us, they shook themselves like dogs, began removing their capes and mopping their streaming faces. 'She all right?' one of them asked, nodding towards Jilly.

'Yes. She's just tired.'

'Wild day,' said another. 'How far you come? That's a nice bike.'

'I'm just borrowing it. It belongs to someone to do with the Luton Twelve.'

'You coming in with us?'

'In?'

'The house. The geezer in the car said to go in and get dry.'

'But it's almost stopped raining now.'

'Yeah. Look bad though, not to go in. After he said.'

They were skinny little people with faces narrowed by continuous slip-stream, eyes sharp like birds' eyes, sinews like cords. Under their capes they wore brilliant proud colours – orange and scarlet and green. Motley, international people. 'Come on. You come on in too.' They made off towards the farmhouse.

'Shall I?' I went over to Jilly as she sat with her back to me. 'Shall I go in with them, Jilly?'

All she did was pass me the note she'd written. On the outside of it she'd scrawled 'Bevis', the tail of the *s* curled down like a tendril and crossed at the end with a kiss.

'Read it if you like.'

'No. I don't.'

'Read it. I mean it. Give it to him. He'll know it the minute he sees it. I used to leave one for him like this every day. In the rabbit hutches. Until they found one.'

I read it. It said, 'I'm in the hay barn – Jilly.'
'Give it to him. Go on. You'll be too late.'

Someone had in fact already shut the front door behind the last of the cyclists when I reached it and I had to bang hard and at once or I should have faltered. It was immediately opened by a fiftyish sort of man who stood smiling at me. He was shortish, squarish and older than Dad had been but there was a sweet, calm presence all around him as he looked down affectionately at me as I stood soaked through and silent at his door.

'Hullo. One more. Come in. Come in. We're just back from the sea and you look as though you've been in it.' He stood back to let me pass down the flagstones, wetted ahead of me by all the cyclists' feet. 'Come along through, my dear. Get warm. There'll be a fire in a minute, but come and stand by the stove first. Are you the last of them?' He peered across the yard.

I couldn't stop looking at him. For the first time since I was a child I wanted to reach out and touch someone. I remembered the feel of my father's clothes again. Such strength, such kindness. Good heavens – old, *old*. And yet I could see the comfort of his arms folding themselves round damaged Jilly. I saw her beautiful head on his shoulder in the house with the Grecian ladies engraved upon the finger-plates; and the fireplaces traced with daffodils.

Then his wife came up alongside and put a hand on his arm. She was a square woman, short, with wiry hair. She was powerful. As powerful as Caesar's wife, as powerful as Volumnia. Her eyes shone.

'Excuse me, dear,' she said to me, and then to him,

'Come in quickly. Great news. *Great* news,' and a sound came floating from a room down the passage that made one think of goals being scored and tidal applause. A wimpish boy and a solid girl came forward flapping letters and the girl flung herself upon her father who swung her round and then put his arm round the boy as well. He hugged both his children together. '*Well!*' said Volumnia to everyone, and the cyclists all gazed. 'Well, we've come home in style. It's the examination results and we have two heroes. *Heroes!*' She shone with such pride she looked beautiful.

'On the mat,' the boy shouted, waving the letter, 'On the mat. I knew they'd be waiting on the mat. And there they were – yooh, hooh!' The girl was giving long silly shrieks and had laid herself along a window-seat.

'What they on about?' one of the cyclists asked me and I said, 'She's happy. Some girls at school do it.'

'Straight A's,' said the lovely father. 'Straight A's for both of them. Two people climbing to the top of the tree. Right to the top. And all set fair.'

The boy, grinning with happiness, came loping across to me. 'D'you want a towel? Are you cold? D'you want some cocoa?' But all he meant was, 'For me the whole world is set fair.'

The girl went on squealing.

And the sun came out and splashed the wet landscape while the rain still attacked the windows of the house with occasional showers of arrows, as if some ancient little army was bitterly out on the moor. Volumnia led us all to a table in another room and put a bowl of soup in front of each of us as she smiled and smiled. There us all to a table in another room and put a bowl of soup in front of each of us as she smiled and smiled. There was nothing, nothing she would not do today, wrapping us all into her magnificent family, for whom all was set fair.

'Shall I relieve you of that?' I heard his voice say over my shoulder as he leaned forward to put a bread basket on the table. My wrists had been propped on the table edge while I waited to see if we were meant to start in on the soup. My left hand had been holding the note marked 'Bevis', with its kiss. The note was no longer there. It had been tweaked away.

Everyone was talking and laughing, gobbling soup and bread, and the cyclist next to me was saying, 'Did you say you were something to do with the Luton Twelve? I'm really more interested in the Bedford Four.'

And Jilly was in the hay barn. Would Bevis go out to her – oh, would he go?

I said, 'Excuse me,' to the cyclist, slid off my chair and went over towards the kitchen where I saw the man standing gravely beside the stove, with the note. He looked not towards me standing outside the door but at the big, fat bottom of his wife as she bent to the refrigerator: her old back, her grey wire hair. Then, when she straightened up and turned to him, he did the thing that ended everything. He lifted the note and held it out to her.

She put down whatever it was she'd been looking for in the fridge. I think it was cheese. A great slab of violent cheese. She walked towards him, took the note and read it, then they looked hard at each other. The man then touched her shoulder, lifted off the little round lid of the stove by its iron handle, took the note back from her hand and dropped it down in the hot coals. She took his hand and held it against her face and they both smiled.

'Jilly. Jilly – where are you?'

She had scarcely moved.

'Jilly, we've got to go. We'll be late. For the train. It's miles and miles.'

'You've gone white again. Did you give Bevis the note?'

'Yes.'

'Well?'

'I don't know. Jilly – let's go. Why're we sitting in this barn? Jilly – you don't want to get pneumonia.'

'I'm not leaving till I've seen him. He'll come out in a minute.'

'He won't. No – don't look at me. He won't.'

'He read it?'

'Yes, he read it.'

'And – ?'

'Jilly, I want to go home.'

'Not,' she said, gripping my waist and I saw for the first time that she had hands not unlike Auntie Greta's, 'not till you tell me.'

'He threw it in the stove.'

'So that she wouldn't see it?'

'No. She was there. Let go. She saw it too. She read it too.'

They –'

'Yes?' She flung away my wrist and stood up from

29

the hay and the over-large landscape behind looked perfectly right for her. 'Yes?'

'They put it in the stove together. Then they smiled.'

An age later she said lightly, 'Oh, well.'

'OK,' she said. 'Never mind. So what?'

It frightened me more than anything.

'If you like, we could wait a bit, Jilly.'

'No,' she said. 'No, I don't think so.'

Her carthorse sped ahead of my racehorse over the wide terrain. Along the wet purple road we flew, paced to the north by the frontier of the Wall, over moors and hills and dykes and ditches, and back to the present-day country of pits and little houses and hedges and shrubs. 'You'd better dry his bike,' she said.

Mr Bainbridge came out of his house and she undid him with her smile. 'We're just going to dry your lovely bike.'

'Oh, that's all right. I'll see to it. Not necessary at all.'

His blush was dark as potted meat. He pleaded with her for some sign.

None.

Half an hour and we were gone.

Because the Bank Holiday was not over until the following day the train home was practically empty and we sat silent in it as far as Sunderland, a Stygian place the train entered and left through a black tunnel (like life, quoth the preacher), and where Jilly got out and disappeared. She returned, not hurrying – I had been in terror for she had the tickets and the money and knew where we had to change trains – with a big bag of crisps. She ate the crisps slowly, giving none to me, staring out of the window. We were alone until Middlesbrough.

Then she said – still staring out – 'Ever been had?'

'Had?'

'Had.'

'You mean, made to look silly? Yes. All the time. Oh, Jilly!'

'Had, had, had, *had*,' she said. '*Had*, Miss No-secrets Angel. You know perfectly well what I mean.'

'You mean – kissing?'

'*Had*,' she said. 'You know. He *had* me. He had me and had me and had me. Every morning in his bed for weeks and weeks and weeks. He HAD me. And how did he have me, Angel Po-face? How did he have me? Let me count the ways. He begged me and begged me and so in the end I climbed out of my bedroom and into his bedroom next door. Every morning at five o'clock and back at seven and down eating breakfast with Gran and Mam, and then walking down the path either side of the fond hedge – three of them and one of me, and off to the Comp by eight all together. We never said a word in the car.'

'But I can't see how. Did he have a bedroom alone, then?'

'Yes, he had a bedroom alone. Don't you know anything yet?'

I thought, I suppose not. I don't. I don't understand anything at all. It must be because there aren't any men in our house. I didn't know that men don't always sleep with their wives.

'Jilly. Wasn't it – ? Weren't you scared?'

'Getting pregnant? No. I don't know why. He didn't use anything. Why've you got your hands over your ears, take them away. Listen. You have to grow up some time.' I said, 'Sorry,' but I didn't know what I meant.

'And God, was I tired,' she said when we stopped at Cargo Fleet siding. 'Was I tired at school. But I got an A in every subject. My mind was as clear . . .'

'Oh God,' she said, staring at the steelworks through the rain, 'I was so happy.'

At Warrenby some people got into the carriage and I sat looking at the floor. I heard one of them say to Jilly – righteously, fiercely, like Teesside people do – 'What's your little sister crying for?', but Jilly didn't answer.

'One thing, I suppose,' she said to me the following week at school – it was the day before she left; she'd failed the History – 'One thing –' she had come up behind me in the dark part of the corridor outside the Science rooms and caught hold of the back of my tunic. She twisted it and the knickers underneath it till she hurt. 'I suppose you didn't see anything in him, did you? You thought he was nothing. You thought, who could see anything in that little shit?'

'Oh, let go, Jilly.'

'Don't cry,' she said. 'You're always crying.'

I was crying because I'd expected love to be beautiful, but I didn't say so.

'Come on, then,' she said. 'Let's hear it. What did you think of him?'

I said, 'He was wonderful.'

*

Jilly died at forty-two, suddenly in Rome. A brain haemorrhage. Something flicked across a lifeline and she was gone. She had not become a vet. She had not even gone to a university. She had gone off on her own at the end of the summer term of the Bank Holiday, first to Paris, where she had become a model for a time. Later she took up with a famous Italian photographer and became a beautiful, known face. There were a few films and then one lavish one that for a short moment gave her face to the whole world. The tawny hair blew out beside autostrade and autoroutes and freeways. The grey eyes stared down at Eros in Piccadilly, at the Corso in Rome, the dust of Athens and the severity of Madrid. But soon it was gone.

Later one kept seeing her in hairdressers' society magazines, always with what is called 'the international set', which is to say, with those whose names are known only to each other (like cyclists). There was a nasty divorce and some hard publicity about money and lovers. But it was not a *louche* life. If anything, I believe it was rather a dry one. She never grew druggy or raddled or mean, and always her face stayed right.

She never came back.

For a while her mother hung about our town but then without warning she moved away too and we heard of her no more. Sometimes my mother said, 'I feel rather bad about Greta. She *is* my sister-in-law. I suppose we could find her. But she never cared for us. And she left no address.'

★

But Jilly and I kept in touch always. We wrote at least six times a year and I heard from her the week before she died. I miss her great scrawl, the fat letters with the foreign stamps, heavy on the mat, although they never really said much.

She died just a month before the Chalmers' grand-child's wedding to which our whole family had been invited, very generously I thought, since we hadn't seen any of them for years. Off we set – my mother and stepfather, me, and my husband and my children in a couple of cars – and very glad to be together for, as my mother said, 'There won't be a soul there we recognize except them and maybe not even them.'

'And the *place*!' she said. 'Just look. Oh, poor Alec – look. All the cobbles have gone. D'you remember all the women on the doorsteps? And the pit-heads and the coal dust?'

Up the slope where we had pushed the bikes between the grim little houses there was only waste land and ruins, boards over windows and notices saying DEMOLI-TION. The Lake District crescents were looking shabby though I thought I saw the box hedge. Only the Chalmers' house, the old rectory over the hill, was bravely surviving beside the unchanged church.

A marquee had been put up on the lawn, approached through the house and the old rector's study. Sensible coconut matting led to the receiving line of the bride and groom. And just beyond this I found myself head-on to Mr and Mrs Bainbridge, looking little changed. They were smiling nervily over their champagne glasses, looking this way and that for a familiar face.

'No, I'm afraid we don't –' Tense, wide smiles.

'You hardly would. I was just thirteen. I borrowed your racing bike, Mr Bainbridge. I was with my cousin, Jilly Willis.'

They seemed delighted with me out of all proportion, swooping forward, almost taking bites out of me. '*Remember!*' they said. 'Remember – of course we do. Remember! *What* a lovely girl!'

'We saw the obituaries,' said Mrs Bainbridge. Mr Bainbridge said, 'Tragic. And so young. It was a great mistake for her to travel.'

'The way she swept off on the bike and never on a racing bike before. Amazing.'

'I often boast about it,' said Mr B, 'that Jilly Willis once borrowed one of my bikes. I still have it hung up in the shed by the old hutches. Out of sentiment for her – and of course for my time with the Luton Twelve.'

'And the Bedford Four,' said his wife.

I introduced them to my mother and heard them saying that of course they understood that she was no relation to the grandmother. No blood relation.

Looking down I found myself staring at the wiry and unthinning hair of Volumnia.

She filled her chair and sat in it as if it were a throne, but there were two sticks with elbow-pieces propped beside her and her feet were swollen round the shoe-straps. She was dancing a small child on her knee.

'Hullo,' she said, looking up at me. 'Now, who are you? I'm afraid I'm rather blind but I know you, don't I? I remember you, I think.'

'You couldn't,' I said. 'We met when I was still a child and now I'm nearly forty. But I recognize you.

We met at your house in the wilds, one wet Bank Holiday.'

'Oh, *that* house,' she said. 'My word, that *was* a romantic house. Very silly. It didn't last long, I'm afraid. Too far out. You must have been a friend of the children – my dear, they're both here. The twins. Both behind you.'

Two indeterminate people were laughing near by and the one who had been the drippish boy looked round – chinless, red-lipped, white-eyelashed. I remembered him at once.

'He became a vet. I expect you knew?' said his mother. 'Doing so well.'

'The day we met he had just passed all his O-levels. It was a very wild, haunted sort of day.'

'Really?' You could see she thought little of the adjective.

'But, how curious . . .' Then she stopped.

'I came in to shelter. I was with my cousin, Jilly Willis. I was with some cyclists. I was Jilly Willis's cousin.'

She looked down at the grandchild on her knee. She bounced him up and down. 'There we are,' she sang. 'There we are.'

'I expect you remember Jilly?'

'That's my baby. Baby boy. Yes, I remember Jilly Willis very well.'

'So do I,' said the son, joining us, wineglass tipping rather. 'Hullo. Who are you? Ought I to know you?'

'I'm Jilly's cousin.'

'I knew Jilly from being a baby,' he said. 'Bloody sad. So young. She was only a few years older than me, you know. We kept rabbits together. It was Jilly started me off wanting to be a vet.' His glass was refilled and he drank. 'Started me off on a lot of things as a matter of fact. Between ourselves.'

'Diddle-de-dee,' sang Volumnia to the baby, 'Bevis, Bevis, Bevis-boy.'

'Is your father here?'

'I'm afraid my father's dead,' he said. 'Do you remember him? Really? Great. Oh, super chap. Lovely man. We miss him.' He drained the glass again.

'Bevis,' I said and saw the sweet-tempered face and Jilly's eyes enlarge with love at the sound of the name. Jilly refusing to mock.

'Yes, Bevis,' he said. 'It's a family name. My son's name.'

'And it was your father's name,' I said.

'Actually, no. No, it wasn't. Dad missed out on Bevis for some reason – he was Rodney. No – I'm Bevis.'

A Friendship

WILLIAM TREVOR

Jason and Ben – fair-haired, ten and eight respectively – found that a bucketful of ready-mixed concrete was too heavy to carry, so they slopped half of it out again. Sharing the handle of the bucket, they found they could now manage to convey their load, even though Ben complained. They carried it from the back yard, through the kitchen and into the hall, to where their father's golf-bag stood in a corner. The bag, recently new, contained driver, putter, mashie and a selection of irons, as well as tees, balls, and gloves in various side pockets. A chair stood in front of the bag, on to which both boys now clambered, still precariously grasping the bucket. They had practised; they knew what they were doing.

After five such journeys the golf-bag was half-full of liquid concrete, the chair carried back to the kitchen, and small splashes wiped from the tiles of the hall. Then the workmen who were rebuilding the boiler shed returned from the Red Lion, where they had spent their lunchtime.

'We know nothing about it,' Jason instructed his brother while they watched the workmen shovelling more sand and cement into the concrete mixer.

'Nothing about it,' Ben obediently repeated.

'Let's go and watch *Quick Draw*.'

'OK.'

When their mother returned to the house half an hour later with her friend Margy, it was Margy who noticed the alien smell in the hall. Being inquisitive by nature she poked about, and was delighted when she discovered the cause since she considered that the victim of the joke would benefit from the inroads it must inevitably make in his pomposity. She propped the front door open for a while so that the smell of fresh concrete would drift away. The boys' mother, Francesca, didn't notice anything.

'Come on!' Francesca called, and the boys came chattering into the kitchen for fish fingers and peas, no yoghurt for Ben because someone had told him it was sour milk, Ribena instead of hot chocolate for Jason.

'You did your homework before you turned on that television?' Francesca asked.

'Yes,' Ben lied.

'I bet you didn't,' Margy said, not looking up from the magazine she was flipping through. Busy with their food, Francesca didn't hear that.

Francesca was tall, with pale, uncurled hair that glistened in the sunlight. Margy was small and dark, brown-eyed, with thin, fragile fingers. They had known one another more or less all their lives.

'Miss Martindale's mother died,' Ben divulged, breaking with the monotony of a silence that had gathered. 'A man interfered with her.'

'My God!' Francesca exclaimed, and Margy closed the magazine, finding little of interest in it.

'Miss Martindale saw him,' Jason said. 'Miss Martindale was just arriving and she saw this figure. First she said a black man, then she said he could be any colour.'

'You mean, Miss Martindale came to school today after something like that?'

'Miss Martindale has a sense of duty,' Jason said.

'Actually, she was extremely late,' Ben said.

'But how ghastly for the poor woman!'

Miss Martindale was a little thing with glasses, Francesca told her friend, not at all up to sustaining something like this. Ben said all the girls had cried, that Miss Martindale herself had cried, that her face was creased and funny because actually she'd been crying all night.

Margy watched Jason worrying in case his brother went too far. They could have said it was Miss Martindale who'd been murdered; they had probably intended to, but had changed it to her mother just in time. It wouldn't have worked if they'd said Miss Martindale because sooner or later Miss Martindale would be there at a parents' evening.

'*Neighbours* now,' Jason said.

'Started actually,' Ben pointed out.

Margy lit a cigarette when she was alone with Francesca, and suggested a drink. She poured gin and Cinzano Bianco for both of them, saying she didn't believe there was much wrong with Miss Martindale's mother, and Francesca, bewildered, looked up from the dishes she was washing. Then, without a word, she left the kitchen and Margy heard her noisily reprimanding her sons, declaring that it was cruel and unfeeling to say people were dead who weren't. Abruptly, the sound of the television ceased and there were footsteps on the stairs. Margy opened a packet of Mignons Morceaux.

When they were two, Francesca and Margy could

43

remember being together in a garden, meeting there for the first time, they afterwards presumed, Francesca smiling, Margy scowling. Later, during their school-days, they had equally disliked a sarcastic teacher with gummy false teeth, and had considered the visiting mathematics man handsome, though neither of them cared for his subject. Later still Francesca became the confidante of Margy's many love affairs, herself confiding from the calmer territory of marriage. Margy brought mild adventure into Francesca's life, and Francesca recognized that Margy would never suffer the loneliness that she feared herself, the vacuum she was certain there would be if her children had not been born. They telephoned one another almost every day, to chat inconsequentially or to break some news, it didn't matter which. Their common ground was the friendship itself: they shared some tastes and some opinions, but only some.

When Philip – father of Jason and Ben – arrived in the house an hour later Francesca and Margy had moved to the sitting-room, taking with them the gin, the Cinzano Bianco, what remained of the Mignons Morceaux, and their glasses.

'Hi, Philip,' Margy greeted him, and watched while he kissed Francesca. He nodded at Margy.

'Margy's going to make us her paella,' Francesca said, and Margy knew that when Philip turned away it was to hide a sigh. He didn't like her paella. He didn't like the herb salad she put together to go with it. He had never said so, being too polite for that, but Margy knew.

'Oh, good,' Philip said.

He hadn't liked the whiff of cigarettes that greeted him when he opened the hall door, or the sound of voices that had come from the sitting-room. He didn't like the crumpled-up Mignons Morceaux packet, the gin bottle and the vermouth bottle on his bureau, Margy's lipstained cigarette-ends, the way Margy was lolling on the floor with her shoes off. Margy didn't have to look to see if this small cluster of aversions registered in Philip's tight features: she knew it didn't; he didn't let things show.

'They've been outrageous,' Francesca said, and began about Miss Martindale's mother.

Margy looked at him then. Nothing moved in his lean face; he didn't blink before he turned away to stand by the open french windows. 'Golf and gardening' he gave as his hobbies in *Who's Who*.

'Outrageous?' he repeated eventually, an inflection in his tone – unnoticed by Francesca – suggesting to Margy that he questioned the use of this word in whatever domestic sense it was being employed. He liked being in *Who's Who*: it was a landmark in his life. One day he would be a High Court judge: everyone said that. One day he would be honoured with a title, and Francesca would be also because she was his wife.

'I was really furious with them,' Francesca said.

He didn't know what all this was about, he couldn't remember who Miss Martindale was because Francesca hadn't said: Margy smiled at her friend's husband, as if to indicate her understanding of his bewilderment, as if in sympathy. It would be the weekend before he discovered that his golf clubs had been set in concrete.

'Be cross with them,' Francesca begged, 'when you

go up. Tell them it was a horrid thing to say about anyone.'

He nodded, his back half-turned on her, still gazing into the garden.

'Have a drink, Philip,' Margy suggested because it was better usually when he had one, though not by much.

'Yes,' Philip said, but instead of going to pour himself something he walked out into the garden.

'I've depressed him,' Francesca commented almost at once. 'He's not in the house more than a couple of seconds and I'm nagging him about the boys.'

She followed her husband into the garden, and a few minutes later, when Margy was gathering together the ingredients for her paella in the kitchen, she saw them strolling among the shrubs he so assiduously tended as a form of relaxation after his week in the courts. The boys would be asleep by the time he went up to say goodnight to them and if they weren't they'd pretend; he wouldn't have to reprimand them about something he didn't understand. Of course all he had to do was to ask a few questions, but he wouldn't because anything domestic was boring for him. It was true that when Mrs Sleet's headscarf disappeared from the back-door pegs he'd asked questions – precise and needling, as if still in one of his court-rooms. And he had reached a conclusion: that the foolish woman must have left her headscarf on the bus. He rejected out of hand Francesca's belief that a passing thief had found the back door open and reached in for what immediately caught his eye. No one would want such an item of clothing, Philip had maintained, no thief in his senses. And of course he was right. Margy remembered the fingernails of the two boys ingrained with earth, and guessed that the head-scarf had been used to wrap up Mabel, Ben's guinea-pig, before confining her to the gerbil and guinea-pig graveyard beside the box hedge.

Smoking while she chopped her herb salad – which he would notice, and silently deplore, as he passed through the kitchen – Margy wondered why Philip's presence grated on her so. He was handsome in his way and strictly speaking he wasn't a bore, nor did he arrogantly impose his views. It was, she supposed, that he was simply a certain kind of man, inimical to those who were not of his ilk, unable to help himself even. Several times at gatherings in this house Margy had met Philip's legal colleagues and was left in no doubt that he was held in high regard, that he commanded both loyalty and respect. Meticulous, fair, precise as a blade, he was feared by his court-room opponents, and professionally he did not have a silly side: in his anticip-ated heights of success, he would surely not become one of those infamous elderly judges who flapped about from court to court, doling out eccentric sentences, lost outside the boundaries of the real world. On the other hand, among a circle of wives and other women of his acquaintance, he was known as 'Bad News', a reference to the misfortune of being placed next to him at a dinner party. On such occasions, when he ran out of his stock of conversational questions he tried no more, and displayed little interest in the small talk that was, increas-ingly desperately, levelled at him. He had a way of saying, flatly, 'I see' when a humorous anecdote, related purely for his entertainment, came to an end. And through all this he was not ill at ease; others laboured, never he.

As Margy dwelt on this catalogue of Philip's favourable and less favourable characteristics, husband and wife passed by the kitchen window. Francesca smiled through the glass at her friend, a way of saying that all was well again after her small *faux pas* of nagging too soon after her husband's return. Then Margy heard the french windows of the sitting-room being closed and Philip's footsteps passed through the hall, on their way to the children's bedroom.

Francesca came in to help, and to open wine. Chatting about other matters, she laid out blue tweed mats on the Formica surface of the table, and forks and other cutlery and glasses. It wasn't so much Philip, Margy thought; had he been married to someone else, she was sure she wouldn't have minded him so. It was the marriage itself: her friend's marriage astonished her.

Every so often Margy and Francesca had lunch at a local bistro called La Trota. It was an elegant rendezvous, though inexpensive and limited in that it offered only fish and a few Italian cheeses. Small and bright and always bustling, its decorative tone was set by a prevalence of aluminium and glass, and matt white surfaces. Its walls were white also, its floor colourfully tiled – a Crustacea pattern that was repeated on the surface of the bar. Two waitresses – one from Sicily, the other from Salerno – served at the tables. Usually, Francesca and Margy had Dover sole and salad, and a bottle of Gavi.

La Trota was in Barnes, not far from Bygone Antiques, where Margy was currently employed. In the mornings Francesca helped in the nearby Little Acorn Nursery School, which both Jason and Ben had attended in the past. Margy worked in Bygone Antiques because she was, 'for the time being' as she put it, involved with its proprietor, who was, as she put it also, 'wearily married'.

On the Tuesday after Philip's discovery of the concrete in his golf-bag they lunched outside, at one of La Trota's three pavement tables, the June day being warm and sunny. Two months ago, when Margy had begun her stint at Bygone Antiques, Francesca was delighted because it meant they would be able to see more of one another: Margy lived some distance away, over the river, in Pimlico.

'He was livid of course,' Francesca reported. 'I mean, they said it was a *joke*.'

Margy laughed.

'I mean, how could it be a joke? And how could it be a joke to say Miss Martindale's mother was dead?'

'Did Mrs Sleet's headscarf ever turn up?'

'You don't think they stole Mrs Sleet's headscarf?'

'What I think is you're lucky to have lively children. Imagine if they never left the straight and narrow.'

'How lovely it would be!'

Francesca told of the quarrel that had followed the discovery of the golf-bag, the worst quarrel of her marriage, she said. She had naturally been blamed because it was clear from what had occurred that the boys had been alone in the house when they shouldn't have been. Philip wanted to know how this had happened, his court-room manner sharpening his questioning and his argument. How long had his children been latchkey children, and for what reason were they so?

'I wish I'd had girls,' Francesca complained pettishly. 'I often think that now.'

Their Dover soles arrived. 'Isn't no help,' the Sicilian waitress muttered crossly as she placed the plates in front of them. 'Every day we say too many tables. Twice times, maybe hundred times. Every day they promise. Next day the same.'

'Ridiculous.' Margy smiled sympathetically at the plump Sicilian girl. 'Poor Francesca,' she sympathized with her friend, taking a piece of lettuce in her fingers.

But Francesca, still lost in the detail of the rumpus there had been, hardly heard. An hour at the very least, Philip was arguing all over again; possibly two hours they must have been on their own. It was absurd to spend all morning looking after children in a nursery school and all afternoon neglecting your own. That Jason and Ben had been sent back early that day, that she had been informed of this beforehand and had forgotten, that she would naturally have been there had she remembered: all this was mere verbiage apparently, not worth listening to, much less considering. Mrs Sleet left the house at one o'clock on the dot, and Francesca was almost always back by three, long before the boys returned. Jason and Ben were not latchkey children; she had made a mistake on a particular day; she had forgotten; she was sorry.

'If you're asked to do anything,' had been the final shaft, 'it's to see to the children, Francesca. You have all the help in the house you ask for. I don't believe you want for much.' The matter of Andy Konig's video had been brought up, and Jason's brazen insistence at the time that it was for Social Studies. Andy Konig's video wouldn't have been discovered if it hadn't become stuck in the video-player, repeating an endless sequence of a woman undressing in a doctor's surgery. 'You didn't even look to see what was on it,' had been the accusation, repeated now, which of course was true. It was over, all this was followed by; they would forget it; he'd drive to the Mortlake tip with the golf-bag, there'd be no television for thirty days, no sweets, cake or biscuits. 'I would ask you to honour that, Francesca.' As the rumpus subsided, she had sniffed back the last of her tears, not replying.

'Oh Lord!' she cried in frustration at La Trota. 'Oh Lord, the guilt!'

Cheering her friend up, Margy insisted that they change the subject. She recounted an episode that morning in the antique shop, a woman she knew quite well, titled actually, slipping a Crown Derby piece into a shopping bag. She touched upon her love affair with the shop's proprietor, which was not going well. One of these days they should look up Sebastian, she idly suggested. 'It's time I settled down,' she murmured over their *cappuccinos*.

'I'm not sure that Sebastian . . .' Francesca began, her concentration still lingering on the domestic upset.

'I often wonder about Sebastian,' Margy said.

Afterwards, in the antique shop, it was cool among the polished furniture, the sofa-tables and revolving libraries, the carved pew ends and sewing cabinets. The collection of early Victorian wall clocks – the speciality of the wearily married proprietor – ticked gracefully; occupying most of the window space, the figure of Christ on a donkey cast shadows that were distorted by the surfaces they reached. A couple in summer clothes, whom Margy had earlier noticed in La Trota, whispered among these offerings. A man with someone else's wife, a wife with someone else's husband: Margy could tell at once. 'Of course,' she'd said when they asked if they might look around, knowing they wouldn't buy anything: people in such circumstances rarely did. 'Oh, isn't that pretty!' the girl whispered now, taken with a framed pot-lid – an 1868 rifle contest in Wimbledon, colourfully depicted.

'Forty-five pounds I think,' Margy replied when she was asked the price, and went away to consult the price book. One day, she believed, Francesca would pay cruelly for her passing error of judgement in marrying the man she had. Hearing about the fuss over the golf-bag, she had felt that instinct justified: the marriage would go from bad to worse, from fusses and quarrels over two little boys' obstreperousness to fusses and quarrels about everything else, a mound of pettiness accumulating, respect all gone and taking with it what once had seemed like love. Too often Margy had heard from married men the kind of bitter talk that was the evidence of this, and had known she would have heard worse still from the wives they spoke of. Yet, just as often, she fairly admitted, people made a go of it. They rarely said so because of course that wasn't interesting, and sometimes what was making a go of it one day was later, in the divorce courts, called tedium.

'Look in again,' she invited the summery couple as they left without the pot-lid.

'Thanks a lot,' the man said, and the girl put her head on one side, a way of indicating, possibly, that she was grateful also.

Margy had mentioned Sebastian at lunch, not because she wished to look him up on her own account but because it occurred to her that Sebastian was just the person to jolly Francesca out of her gloom. Sebastian was given to easy humour and exuded an agreeableness that was pleasant to be exposed to. Since he had once, years ago, wanted to marry Francesca, Margy often imagined what her friend's household would have been like with Sebastian there instead.

'Hullo,' her employer said, entering the shop with a Regency commode and bringing with him the raw scent of the stuff he dabbed on his underarms, and a whiff of beer.

'Handsome,' Margy remarked, referring to the commode.

It was Francesca who telephoned Sebastian. 'A voice from the past,' she said and he knew immediately, answering her by name. He was pleased she'd rung, he said, and all the old telephone inflections, so familiar once, registered again as their conversation progressed. 'Margy?' he repeated when Francesca suggested lunch for three. He sounded disappointed, but Francesca hardly noticed that, caught up with so much else, wondering how in fact it would affect everything if, somehow or other, Sebastian and Margy hit it off now, as she and Sebastian had in the past. She knew Sebastian hadn't married. He had been at her wedding; she would have been at his, their relationship transformed on both sides then. Like Margy, Francesca imagined, Sebastian had free-wheeled through the time that had passed since. At her wedding she had guessed they would lose touch, and in turn probably he had guessed that that was, sensibly, what she wanted. Sebastian, who had never honoured much, honoured that. When marriage occurs, the past clams up, lines are drawn beneath a sub-total.

'Well, well, well,' he murmured at La Trota, embracing Margy first and then Francesca. There were flecks of grey in his fair hair; his complexion was a little ruddier. But his lazy eyes were touched with the humour that both women remembered, and his big hands seemed gentle on the table.

'You haven't changed a bit,' Sebastian said, choosing Francesca to say it to.

'Oh heavens, I've said the wrong thing!' a woman exclaimed in horror at a party, eyes briefly closed, a half-stifled breath drawn in.

'No, not at all,' Philip said.

'It's just that –'

'We see Sebastian quite often, actually.'

He wondered why he lied, and realized then that he was saving face. He had been smiling when the woman first mentioned Sebastian, when she'd asked how he was these days. Almost at once the woman had known she was saying the wrong thing, her expression adding more and more as she stumbled on, endeavouring to muddle with further words her original statement about trying unsuccessfully to catch Francesca's and Sebastian's attention in Wigmore Street.

'So very nice,' the woman floundered, hot-faced. 'Sebastian.'

A mass of odds and ends gathered in Philip's mind. 'The number of this taxi is 22003,' he had said after he'd kissed Francesca in it. Their first embrace, and he had read out the number from the enamel disc on the back of the driver's seat, and neither of them had since forgotten it. The first present Francesca gave him was a book about wine which to this day he wouldn't lend to people.

No one was as honest as Francesca, Philip reflected as the woman blundered on: it was impossible to accept that Francesca had told lies, even through reticence. Yet now there were – as well – the odds and ends of the warm summer that had just passed, all suddenly transformed. Dates and the order of events glimmered in Philip's brain; he was good at speedy calculation and accurately recalling. Excuses, and explanations, seemed elaborate in the bare light of the hindsight that was forced upon him. A note falling to the floor had been too hastily retrieved. There were headaches and cancellations and apologies. There'd been a difference in Francesca that hadn't at the time seemed great but seemed great now.

'Yes, Sebastian's very nice,' Philip said.

'It's over,' Francesca said in their bedroom. 'It's been over for weeks, as a matter of fact.'

Still dressed, sitting on the edge of their bed, Francesca was gazing at the earrings she'd just taken off, two drops of amber in the palm of her hand. Very slowly she made a pattern of them, moving them on her palm with the forefinger of her other hand. In their bedroom the light was dim, coming only from a bedside lamp. Francesca was in the shadows.

'It doesn't make much difference that it's over,' Philip said. 'That's not the point.'

'I know.'

'You've never told lies before.'

'Yes, I know. I hated it.'

Even while it was happening, she had sometimes thought it wasn't. And for the last few lonely weeks it had felt like madness, as indeed it had been. Love was madness of a kind, Margy had said once, years ago, and Francesca at that time hadn't understood: being fond of Sebastian in the past, and loving Philip, she had never been touched by anything like that. Her recent inexplicable aberration felt as if she had taken time off from being herself, and now was back again where she belonged, not understanding, as bouts of madness are never understood.

'That's hardly an explanation,' her husband said when she endeavoured to relate some of this.

'No, I know it isn't. I would have told you about it quite soon; I couldn't not tell you.'

'I didn't even notice I wasn't loved.'

'You are loved, Philip. I ended it. And besides, it wasn't much.'

A silence grew between them. 'I love you,' Sebastian had said no longer ago than last June, and in July and in August and September also. And she had loved him too. More than she loved anyone else, more than she loved her children: that thought had been there. Yet now she could say it wasn't much.

As though he guessed some part of this, Philip said: 'I'm dull compared to him. I'm grey and dull.'

'No.'

'I mooch about the garden, I mooch about on golf courses. You've watched me becoming greyer in middle age. You don't want to share our middle age.'

'I never think things like that. Never, Philip.'

'No one respects a cuckold.'

Francesca did not reply. She was asked if she wanted a divorce. She shook her head.

Philip said: 'One day in the summer you and Margy were talking about a key when I came in, and you stopped and said: "Have a drink, darling?" I remember now. Odd, how stuff's dredged up. The key to Margy's flat, I think?'

Francesca stood up. She placed her amber earrings in the drawer of their bedside table and slowly began to undress. Philip, standing by the door, said he had always trusted her, which he had said already.

'I'm sorry I hurt you, Philip.' Tiredly, she dropped into a cliché, saying that Sebastian had been exorcized as a ghost is exorcized, that at last she had got him out of her system. But what she said had little relevance, and mattered so slightly that it was hardly heard. What was there between them were the weekends Philip had been in charge of the children because Francesca needed a rest and had gone, with Margy, to some seaside place where Margy was looking after a house for people who were abroad. And the evenings she helped to paint Margy's flat. And the mornings that were free after she gave up helping in the Little Acorn Nursery School. Yes, that key had been Margy's, Francesca said. Left for her under a stone at the foot of a hydrangea bush in Pimlico, in a block of flats' communal garden: she didn't add that. Found there with a *frisson* of excitement: nor that either.

'I'm ashamed because I hurt you,' she said instead. 'I'm ashamed because I was selfish and a fool.'

'You should have married him in the first place.'

'It was you I wanted to marry, Philip.'

Francesca put on her nightdress, folded her underclothes, and draped her tights over the back of a chair. She sat for a moment in front of her dressing-table looking-glass, rubbing cold cream into her face, stroking away the moisture of tears.

'You have every right to turn me out,' she said, calmly now. 'You have every right to have the children to yourself.'

'D'you want that?'

'No.'

He hated her, Francesca thought, but she sensed as well that this hatred was a visitation only, that time would take it away. And she guessed that Philip sensed this also, and resented it that something as ordinary as passing time could destroy the high emotions he was experiencing now. Yet it was the truth.

'It happened by chance,' Francesca said, and made it all sound worse. 'I thought that Margy and Sebastian – oh well, it doesn't matter.'

They quarrelled then. The tranquillity that had prevailed was shattered in a moment, and their children woke and heard the raised voices. Underhand, hole-in-corner, shabby, untrustworthy, dishonourable, grubby: these words had never described Francesca in the past, but before the light of morning they were used. And to add a garnish to all that was said, there was Margy's treachery too. She had smiled and connived even though there was nothing in it for her.

Francesca countered when her spirit returned, after she'd wept beneath this lash of accusation, and the condemnation of her friend. Philip had long ago withdrawn himself from the family they were; it was an irony that her misbehaviour had pulled him back, that occasionally he had had to cook beans and make the bacon crispy for their children, and see that their rooms were tidied, their homework finished. At least her lies had done that.

But there was no forgiveness when they dressed again. Nothing was over yet. Forgiveness came later.

There was a pause after Francesca made her bleak statement in La Trota. Margy frowned, beginning to lean across the table because the hubbub was considerable that day. No longer working at Bygone Antiques, she had come across London specially.

'Drop me?' Margy said, and Francesca nodded: that was her husband's request.

The restaurant was full of people: youngish, well-to-do, men together, women together, older women with older men, older men with girls, five businessmen at a table. The two waitresses hurried with their orders, too busy to mutter their complaints about the over-crowding.

'But why on earth?' Margy said. 'Why should you?'

Expertly, the Sicilian waitress opened the Gavi and splashed some into their glasses. '*Buon appetito*,' she briskly wished them, returning in a moment with the sole. They hadn't spoken since Margy had asked her questions.

'He has a right to something, is that it?' Margy squeezed her chunk of lemon over the fish and then on to her salad. 'To punish?'

'He thinks you betrayed him.'

'*I* betrayed him? *I*?'

'It's how Philip feels. No, not a punishment,' Francesca said. 'Philip's not doing that.'

'What, then?'

Francesca didn't reply, and Margy poked at the fish on her plate, not wanting to eat it now. Some vague insistence hovered in her consciousness: some truth, not known before and still not known, was foggily sensed.

'I don't understand this,' Margy said. 'Do you?'

A salvaging of pride was a wronged husband's due; she could see that and could understand it, but there was more to this than pride.

'It's how Philip feels,' Francesca said again. 'It's how all this has left him.'

She knew, Margy thought: whatever it was, it had been put to Francesca in Philip's court-room manner, pride not even mentioned. Then, about to ask and before she could, she knew herself: the forgiving of a wife was as much as there could be. How could a wronged husband, so hurt and so aggrieved, forgive a treacherous friend as well?

'Love allows forgiveness,' Francesca said, guessing what Margy's thoughts were, which was occasionally possible after years of intimacy.

But Margy's thoughts were already moving on. Every time she played with his children he would remember the role she had played that summer; she could hear him saying it, and Francesca's silence. Every present she brought to the house would seem to him to be a traitor's bribe. The summer would always be there, embalmed in the friendship that had made the deception possible – the key to the flat, the seaside house, the secret kept and then discovered. What the marriage sought to forget the friendship never would because the summer had become another part of it. The friendship could only be destructive now, the subject of argument and quarrels, the cause of jealousy and pettiness and distress. This Philip presented as his case, his logic perfect in all its parts. And again Margy could hear his voice.

'It's unfair, Francesca.'

'It only seems so.' Francesca paused, then said: 'I love Philip, you know.'

'Yes, I do know.'

In the crowded bistro their talk went round in muddled circles, the immediacy of the blow that had been struck at them lost from time to time in the web of detail that was their friendship, lost in days and moments and occasions not now recalled but still remembered, in confidences, and conversation rattling on, in being different in so many ways and that not mattering. Philip, without much meaning to, was offering his wife's best friend a stature she had not possessed before in his estimation: she was being treated with respect. But that, of course, was neither here nor there.

'What was her name,' Margy asked, 'that woman with the gummy teeth?'

'Hyatt. Miss Hyatt.'

'Yes, of course it was.'

There was a day when Margy was cross and said

Francesca was not her friend and never would be, when they were six. There was the time the French girl smoked when they were made to take her for a walk on the hills behind their boarding-school. Margy fell in love with the boy who brought the papers round. Francesca's father died and Margy read Tennyson to cheer her up. They ran out of money on their cycling tour and borrowed from a lorry driver who got the wrong idea. Years later Francesca was waiting afterwards when Margy had her abortion.

'You like more *cappuccinos*?' the Sicilian waitress offered, placing fresh cups of coffee before them because they always had two each.

'Thanks very much,' Francesca said.

In silence, in the end, they watched the bistro emptying. The two waitresses took the tablecloths off and lifted the chairs on to the tables in order to mop over the coloured patterns of fish on the tiled floor. Quite suddenly a wave of loneliness caused Margy to shiver inwardly, as the chill news of death does.

'Perhaps with a bit of time,' she began, but even as she spoke she knew that time would make no difference. Time would simply pass, and while it did so Francesca's guilt would still be there; she would always feel she owed this sacrifice. They would not cheat; Francesca would not do that a second time. She would say that friends meeting stealthily was ridiculous, a grimier deception than that of lovers.

'It's all my fault,' Francesca said.

Hardly perceptibly, Margy shook her head, knowing it wasn't. She had gone too far; she had been sillily angry because of a children's prank. She hadn't sought

62

to knock a marriage about, only to give her friend a treat that seemed to be owing to her, only to rescue her for a few summer months from her exhausting children and her exhausting husband, from Mrs Sleet and the Little Acorn Nursery School, from her too-safe haven. But who was to blame, and what intentions there had been, didn't matter in the least now.

'In fairness,' Francesca said, 'Philip has a point of view. Please say you see it, Margy.'

'Oh yes, I see it.' She said it quickly, knowing she must do so before it became impossible to say, before all generosity was gone. She knew, too, that one day Francesca would pass on this admission to her husband because Francesca was Francesca, who told the truth and was no good at deception.

'See you soon,' the Sicilian waitress called out when eventually they stood up to go.

'Yes,' Margy agreed, lying for her friend as well. On the pavement outside La Trota they stood for a moment in a chill November wind, then moved away in their two different directions.

The Candle Maker

ROSE TREMAIN

For thirty-three years, Mercedes Dubois worked in a laundry.

The laundry stood on a west-facing precipice in the hilltop town of Leclos. It was one of the few laundries in Corsica with a view of the sea.

On fine evenings, ironing at sunset was a pleasant – almost marvellous – occupation and for thirty-three years Mercedes Dubois considered herself fortunate in her work. To her sister, Honorine, who made paper flowers, she remarked many times over the years: 'In my work, at least, I'm a fortunate woman.' And Honorine, twisting wire, holding petals in her mouth, always muttered: 'I don't know why you have to put it like that.'

Then the laundry burned down.

The stone walls didn't burn, but everything inside them turned to black iron and black oil and ash. The cause was electrical, so the firemen said. Electricians in Leclos, they said, didn't know how to earth things properly.

The burning down of the laundry was the second tragedy in the life of Mercedes Dubois. She didn't know how to cope with it. She sat in her basement apartment and stared at her furniture. It was a cold

December and Mercedes was wearing her old red anorak. She sat with her hands in her anorak pockets, wondering what she could do. She knew that in Leclos, once a thing was lost, it never returned. There had been a bicycle shop once, and a library and a lacemaker's. There had been fifty children and three teachers at the school; now, there were twenty children and one teacher. Mercedes pitied the lone teacher, just as she pitied the mothers and fathers of all the schoolchildren who had grown up and gone away. But there was nothing to be done about any of it. Certainly nothing one woman, single all her life, could do. Better not to remember the variety there had been. And better, now, not to remember the sunset ironing or the camaraderie of the mornings, making coffee, folding sheets. Mercedes Dubois knew that the laundry would never reopen because it had never been insured. Sitting with her hands in her anorak pockets, staring at her sideboard, was all there was to be done about it.

But after a while she stood up. She went over to the sideboard and poured herself a glass of anisette. She put it on the small table where she ate her meals and sat down again and looked at it. She thought: I can drink the damned anisette. I can do that at least.

She had always considered her surname right for her. She was as hard as wood. Wood, not stone. She could be pliant. And once, long ago, a set of initials had been carved on her heart of wood. It was after the carving of these initials that she understood how wrong for her first name was. She had been christened after Our Lady of Mercy, Maria de las Mercedes, but she had been unable to show mercy. On the contrary, what had consumed her was despair and malevolence. She had lain in her iron bed and consoled herself with thoughts of murder.

Mercedes Dubois: stoical but without forgiveness; a woman who once planned to drown her lover and his new bride and instead took a job in a laundry; what could she do, now that the laundry was gone?

To her sister, Honorine, she asked the question: 'What can anyone do in so terrible a world?'

And Honorine replied: 'I've been wondering about that, because, look at my hands. I've got the beginnings of arthritis, see? I'm losing my touch with the paper flowers.'

'There you are,' said Mercedes. 'I don't know what anyone can do except drink.'

But Honorine, who was married to a sensible man, a plasterer, shook a swollen finger at her sister and warned: 'Don't go down that road. There's always something. That's what we've been taught to believe. Why don't you go and sit in the church and think about it?'

'Have *you* gone and sat in the church and thought about it?' asked Mercedes.

'Yes.'

'And?'

'I noticed all the flowers in there are plastic these days. It's more durable than paper. We're going to save up and buy the kind of machinery you need to make a plastic flower.'

Mercedes left Honorine and walked down the dark, steep street, going towards home and the anisette bottle. She was fifty-four years old. The arrival of this second catastrophe in her life had brought back her memories of the first.

The following day, obedient to Honorine, she went into the Church of St Vida, patron saint of lemon growers, and walked all around it very slowly, wondering where best to sit and think about her life. Nowhere seemed best. To Mercedes the child, this church had smelled of satin; now it smelled of dry rot. Nobody cared for it. Like the laundry, it wasn't insured against calamity. And the stench of calamity was here. St Vida's chipped plaster nostrils could detect it. She stood in her niche, holding a lemon branch to her breast, staring pitifully down at her broken foot. Mercedes thought: poor Vida, what a wreck, and no lemon growers left in Leclos. What can either Vida or I do in so desolate a world?

She sat in a creaking pew. She shivered. She felt a simple longing, now, for something to warm her while she thought about her life, so she went to where the votive candles flickered on their iron sconces – fourteen of them on the little unsteady rack – and warmed her hands there.

There was only one space left for a new candle and Mercedes thought: this is what the people of Leclos do in answer to loss: they come to St Vida's and light a candle. When the children leave, when the bicycle shop folds, when the last lacemaker dies, they illuminate a little funnel of air. It costs a franc. Even Honorine, saving up for her plastics machine, can afford one franc. And the candle is so much more than itself. The candle is the voice of a lover, the candle is a catch of mackerel, the candle is a drench of rain, a garden of marrows, a neon sign, a year of breath . . .

So Mercedes paid a franc and took a new candle and lit it and put it in the last vacant space on the rack. She admired it possessively: its soft colour, its resemblance to something living. But what *is* it? she asked herself. What *is* my candle? If only it could be something as simple as rain!

At this moment, the door of St Vida's opened and Mercedes heard footsteps go along the nave. She turned and recognized Madame Picaud, proprietor of the lost laundry. This woman had once been a café singer in Montparnasse. She'd worn feathers in her hair. On the long laundry afternoons, she used to sing ballads about homesickness and the darkness of bars. Now, she'd lost her second livelihood and her head was draped in a shawl.

Madame Picaud stood by the alcove of St Vida, looking up at the lemon branch and the saint's broken foot. Mercedes was about to slip away and leave the silence of the church to her former employer, when she had a thought that caused her sudden and unexpected distress: suppose poor Madame Picaud came, after saying a prayer to Vida, to light a candle and found that there was no space for it in the rack? Suppose Madame Picaud's candle was a laundry rebuilt and re-equipped with new, bright windows looking out at the ocean? Suppose the future of Madame Picaud – with which her own future would undoubtedly be tied – rested upon the ability of this single tongue of yellow fire to burn unhindered in the calamitous air of the Church of St Vida? And then it could not burn. It could not burn because there were too many other futures already up there flickering away on the rack.

Mercedes looked at her own candle and then at all the others. Of the fifteen, she judged that five or six had been burning for some time. And so she arrived at a decision about these: they were past futures. They had had their turn. What counted was the moment of lighting, or, if not merely the moment of lighting, then the moment of lighting and the first moments of burning. When the candles got stubby and started to burn unevenly, dripping wax into the tray, they were no longer love letters or olive harvests or cures for baldness or machines that manufactured flowers; they were simply old candles. They had to make way. No one had understood this until now. *I* understand it, said Mercedes to herself, because I know what human longing there is in Leclos. I know it because I am part of it.

She walked round to the back of the rack. She removed the seven shortest candles and blew them out. She rearranged the longer candles, including her own, until the seven spaces were all at the front, inviting seven new futures, one of which would be Madame Picaud's.

Then Mercedes walked home with the candles stuffed into the pockets of her red anorak. She laid them out on her table and looked at them.

She had never been petty or underhand.

She went to see the Curé the following morning and told him straight out that she wanted to be allowed to keep the future burning in Leclos by recycling the votive candles. She said: 'With the money you save, you could restore St Vida's foot.'

The Curé offered Mercedes a glass of wine. He had a fretful smile. He said: 'I've heard it's done elsewhere, in the great cathedrals, where they get a lot of tourists, but it's never seemed necessary in Leclos.'

Mercedes sipped her wine. She said: 'It's *more* necessary here than in Paris or Reims, because hope stays alive much longer in those places. In Leclos, everything vanishes. Everything.'

The Curé looked at her kindly. 'I was very sorry to hear about the laundry,' he said. 'What work will you do now?'

'I'm going to do this,' said Mercedes. 'I'm going to do the candles.'

He nodded. 'Fire, in Corsica, has always been an enemy. But I expect Madame Picaud had insurance against it?'

'No, she didn't,' said Mercedes, 'only the free kind: faith and prayer.'

The Curé finished his glass of wine. He shook his head discreetly, as if he were a bidder at an auction who has decided to cease bidding.

'I expect you know,' he said after a moment, 'that the candles have to be of a uniform size and length?'

'Oh, yes.'

'And I should add that if there *are* savings of any import . . . then . . .'

'I don't want a few francs, Monsieur le Curé. I'm not interested in that. I just want to make more room for something to happen here, that's all.'

Collecting the candles and melting them down began to absorb her. She put away the anisette bottle. She went into the church at all hours. She was greedy for the candles. So she began removing even those that had burned for only a short time. She justified this to herself by deciding, once and for ever, that what mattered in every individual wish or intention was the act of lighting the candle – the moment of illumination. This alone. Nothing else. And she watched what people did. They lit their candles and looked at them for no more than a minute. Then they left. They didn't keep on returning to make sure their candles were still alight.

'The point is,' Mercedes explained to Honorine, 'they continue to burn in the imagination and the value you could set on the imagination would be higher than one franc. So the actual life of the candle is of no importance.'

'How can you be sure?' asked Honorine.

'I am sure. You don't need to be a philosopher to see it.'

'And what if a person did come back to check her individual candle?'

'The candles are identical, Honorine. A field of basil is indistinguishable from an offer of marriage.'

She had ordered six moulds from the forge and sent off for a hundred metres of cotton wick from a maker of night-lights in Ajaccio. The smell of bubbling wax pervaded her apartment. It resembled the smell of new leather, pleasant yet suffocating.

She began to recover from her loss of the job at the laundry. Because, in a way, she thought, I've *become* a laundry; I remove the soiled hopes of the town and make them new and return them neatly to the wooden candle drawer.

The Social Security office paid her a little sum of money each week. She wasn't really poor, not as poor as she'd feared, because her needs were few.

Sometimes, she walked out to the coast road and looked at the black remains of what had been spin driers and cauldrons of bleach, and then out beyond the pile of devastation to the sea, with its faithful mirroring of the sky and its indifference. She began to smell the spring on the salt winds.

News, in Leclos, travelled like fire. It leapt from threshold to balcony, from shutter to shutter.

One morning, it came down to Mercedes's door: 'Someone has returned, Mercedes. You can guess who.'

Mercedes stood in her doorway, blinking into the February sun. The bringer of the news was Honorine. Honorine turned and went away up the street leaving Mercedes standing there. The news burned in her throat. She said his name: Louis Cabrini.

She had believed he would never return to Leclos. He'd told her thirty-three years ago that he'd grown to dislike the town, dislike the hill it sat on, dislike its name and its closed-in streets. He said: 'I've fallen in love, Mercedes – with a girl and with a place. I'm going to become a Parisian now.'

He had married his girl. She was a ballerina. Her name was Sylvie. It was by her supple, beautiful feet that the mind of Mercedes Dubois chained her to the ocean bed. For all that had been left her after Louis went away were her dreams of murder. Because she'd known, from the age of twenty that she, Mercedes, was going to be his wife. She had known and all of Leclos had known: Louis Cabrini and Mercedes Dubois were meant for each other. There would be a big wedding at the Church of St Vida and, after that, a future . . .

Then he went to Paris, to train as an engineer. He met a troupe of dancers in a bar. He came back to Leclos just the one time, to collect his belongings and say goodbye to Mercedes. He had stood with her in the square and it had been a sunny February day – a day just like this one, on which Honorine had brought the news of his return – and after he'd finished speaking, Mercedes walked away without a word. She took twelve steps and then she turned round. Louis was standing quite still, watching her. He had taken her future away and this was all he could do – stand still and stare. She said: 'I'm going to kill you, Louis. You and your bride.'

Mercedes went down into her apartment. A neat stack of thirty candles was piled up on her table, ready to be returned to St Vida's. A mirror hung above the sideboard and Mercedes walked over to it and looked at herself. She had her father's square face, his deep-set brown eyes, his wiry hair. And his name. She would stand firm in the face of Honorine's news. She would go about her daily business in Leclos as if Louis were not there. If she chanced to meet him, she would pretend she hadn't recognized him. He was older than she was. He might by now, with his indulgent Parisian life, look like an old man. His walk would be slow.

But then a new thought came: suppose he hadn't returned to Leclos alone, as she'd assumed? Suppose when Mercedes went to buy her morning loaf, she had to meet the fading beauty of the ballerina? And hear her addressed as Madame Cabrini? And see her slim feet in expensive shoes?

Mercedes put on her red anorak and walked up to Honorine's house. Honorine's husband, Jacques the plasterer, was there and the two of them were eating their mid-day soup in contented silence.

'You didn't tell me,' said Mercedes. 'Has he come back alone?'

'Have some soup,' said Jacques. 'You look pale.'

'I'm not hungry,' said Mercedes. 'I need to know, Honorine.'

'All I've heard is rumour,' said Honorine.

'Well?'

'They say she left him. Some while back. They say he's been in poor health ever since.'

Mercedes nodded. Not really noticing what she did, she sat down at Honorine's kitchen table. Honorine and Jacques put down their spoons and looked at her. Her face was waxy. They thought she was going to faint.

Jacques said: 'Give her some soup, Honorine.' Then he said: 'There's too much history in Corsica. It's in the stone.'

When Mercedes left Honorine's she went straight to the church. On the way, she kept her head down and just watched her shadow moving along ahead of her.

There was nobody in St Vida's. Mercedes went straight to the candle sconces. She snatched up two low-burning candles and blew them out. She stood still a moment, hesitating. Then she blew out all the remaining candles. It's wretched, wretched, she thought: all this interminable flickering optimistic light; wretched beyond comprehension.

After February, in Corsica, the spring comes fast. The *maquis* starts to bloom. The mimosas come into flower.

Mercedes was susceptible to the perfume of things.

So this year, she didn't want even to *see* the mimosa blossom. She wanted everything to stay walled up in its own particular winter. She wanted clouds to gather and envelop the town in a dark mist.

She crept about the place like a thief. She had no conversations. She scuttled here and there, not looking, not noticing. In her apartment, she kept the shutters closed. She worked on the candles by the light of a single bulb.

Honorine came down to see her. 'You can't go on like this, Mercedes,' she said. 'You can't live this way.'

'Yes, I can,' said Mercedes.

'He looks old,' said Honorine, 'his skin's yellowy. He's not the handsome person he used to be.'

Mercedes said nothing. She thought, no one in this place, not even my sister, has ever understood what I feel.

'You ought to go and meet him,' said Honorine. 'Have a drink with him. It's time you forgave him.'

Mercedes busied herself with the wax she was melting in a saucepan. She turned her back towards Honorine.

'Did you hear what I said?' asked Honorine.

'Yes,' said Mercedes, 'I heard.'

After Honorine had left, Mercedes started to weep. Her tears fell into the wax and made it spit. Her cheeks were pricked with small burns. She picked up a kitchen cloth and buried her head in it. She thought, what no one understands is that this darkness isn't new. I've been in it in my mind for thirty-three years, ever since that February morning in the square when the mimosas were coming into flower. There were moments when it lifted – when those big sunsets came in at the laundry window, for instance – but it always returned, as night follows day; always and always.

And then she thought, but Honorine is right, it is intolerable. I should have done what I dreamed of doing. I should have killed him. Why was I so cowardly? I should have cut off his future – all those days and months of his happy life in Paris that I kept seeing like a film in my head: the ballerina's hair falling on his body; her feet touching his feet under the dainty patis- serie table; their two summer shadows moving over the water of the Seine. I should have ended it as I planned, and then I would have been free of him and out of the darkness and I could have had a proper life.

And now. There she was in Leclos, in her own town that she'd never left, afraid to move from her flat, gliding to and from the church like a ghost, avoiding every face, sunk into a loneliness so deep and fast it resembled the grave. Was this how the remainder of her life was to be spent?

She prised the buttons of wax from her cheeks with her finger-nails. She took the saucepan off the gas flame and laid it aside, without pouring its contents into the candle moulds. It was a round-bottomed pan and Mer- cedes could imagine the smooth, rounded shape into which the wax would set.

She ran cold water on to her face, drenching her hair, letting icy channels of water eddy down her neck and touch her breasts. Her mind had recovered from its futile weeping and had formulated a plan and she wanted to feel the chill of the plan somewhere near her heart.

★

She lay awake all night. She had decided to kill Louis Cabrini.

Not with her own hands, face to face. Not like that.

She would do it slowly. From a distance. With all the power of the misery she'd held inside her for thirty-three years.

Morning came and she hadn't slept. She stared at the meagre strips of light coming through the shutters. In this basement apartment, it was impossible to gauge what kind of day waited above. But she knew that what waited above, today, was the plan. It was Friday. In Mercedes' mind, the days of the week were different colours. Wednesday was red. Friday was a pallid kind of yellow.

She dressed and put on her apron. She sat at her kitchen table drinking coffee and eating bread. She heard two women go past her window, laughing. She thought: that was the other beautiful thing that happened in the laundry – laughter.

When the woman had walked on by and all sound of them had drained away, Mercedes said aloud: 'Now.'

She cleared away the bread and coffee. She lit one ring of the stove and held above it the saucepan full of wax, turning it like a chef turns an omelette pan, so that the flames spread an even heat round the body of the wax. She felt it come loose from the saucepan, a solid lump. 'Good,' she said.

She set out a pastry board on the table. She touched its smooth wooden surface with her hand. Louis Cabrini had been childishly fond of pastries and cakes. In her mother's kitchen, Mercedes used to make him *tarte tatin* and apfelstrudel.

She turned out the lump of wax on to the pastry board. It was yellowy in colour. The more she recycled the candles the yellower they became.

Now she had a round dome of wax on which to begin work.

She went to the bookcase, which was almost empty except for a green, chewed set of the collected works of Victor Hugo. Next to Hugo was a book Mercedes had borrowed from the library thirty-three years ago to teach herself about sex and had never returned, knowing perhaps that the library, never very efficient with its reminders, would close in due time. It was called *Simple Anatomy of the Human Body*. It contained drawings of all the major internal organs. On page fifty-nine was a picture of the male body unclothed, at which Mercedes used to stare.

Mercedes put the book next to the pastry board, under the single light. She turned the pages until she found the drawing of the heart. The accompanying text read: 'The human heart is small, relative to its import- ance. It is made up of four chambers, the right and left auricle and the right and left ventricle . . .'

'All right,' said Mercedes.

Using the drawing as a guide, she began to sculpt a heart out of the wax dome. She worked with a thin filleting knife and two knitting-needles of different gauges.

Her first thought as she started the sculpture was: the thing it most resembles is a fennel root and the smell of fennel resembles in its turn the smell of anisette.

The work absorbed her. She didn't feel tired any more. She proceeded carefully and delicately, striving for verisimilitude. She knew that this heart was larger than a heart is supposed to be and she thought, well, in Louis Cabrini's case, it swelled with pride – pride in his beautiful wife, pride in his successful career, pride in being a Parisian, at owning a second-floor apartment, at eating in good restaurants, at buying roses at dusk to take home to his woman. Pride in leaving Leclos behind. Pride in his ability to forget the past.

She imagined his rib-cage expanding to accommodate this swollen heart of his.

Now and again, she made errors. Then she had to light a match and pass it over the wax to melt it – to fill too deep an abrasion or smooth too jagged an edge. And she noticed in time that this slight re-melting of the heart gave it a more liquid, living appearance. This was very satisfactory. She began to relish it. She would strike a match and watch an ooze begin, then blow it out and slowly repair the damage she'd caused.

It was becoming, just as she'd planned, her plaything. Except that she'd found more ways to wound it than she'd imagined. She had thought that, in the days to come, she would pierce it or cut it with something – scissors, knives, razor-blades. But now she remembered that its very substance was unstable. She could make it bleed. She could make it disintegrate. It could empty itself out. And then, if she chose, she could rebuild it, make it whole again. She felt excited and hot. She thought: I have never had power over anything; this has been one of the uncontrovertible facts of my life.

As the day passed and darkness filled the cracks in the shutters, Mercedes began to feel tired. She moved the anatomy book aside and laid her head on the table beside the pastry board. She put her hand inside her grey shirt and squeezed and massaged her nipple, and her head filled with dreams of herself as a girl, standing in the square, smelling the sea and smelling the mimosa blossom, and she fell asleep.

She thought someone was playing a drum. She thought there was a march coming up the street.

But it was a knocking on her door.

She raised her head from the table. Her cheek was burning hot from lying directly under the light-bulb. She had no idea whether it was night-time yet. She remembered the heart, almost finished, in front of her. She thought the knocking on her door would be Honorine coming to talk to her again and tell her she couldn't go on living the way she was.

She didn't want Honorine to see the heart. She got up and draped a clean tea-towel over it, as though it were a newly baked cake. All around the pastry board were crumbs of wax and used matches. Mercedes tried to sweep them into her hand and throw them in the sink. She felt dizzy after her sleep on the table. She staggered about like a drunk. She knew she'd been having beautiful dreams.

When she opened the door, she saw a man standing there. He wore a beige mackintosh and a yellow scarf. Underneath the mackintosh, his body looked bulky. He wore round glasses. He said: 'Mercedes?'

She put a hand up to her red burning cheek. She blinked at him. She moved to close the door in his face, but he anticipated this and put out a hand, trying to keep the door open.

'Don't do that,' he said. 'That's the easy thing to do.'

'Go away,' said Mercedes.

'Yes. OK. I will, I promise. But first let me in. Please. Just for ten minutes.'

Mercedes thought: if I didn't feel so dizzy, I'd be stronger. I'd be able to push him out. But all she did was hold on to the door and stare at him. Louis Cabrini. Wearing glasses. His curly hair getting sparse. His belly fat.

He came into her kitchen. The book of human anatomy was still open on the table, next to the covered heart.

He looked all around the small, badly lit room. From his mackintosh pocket, he took out a bottle of red wine and held it out to her. 'I thought we could drink some of this.'

Mercedes didn't take the bottle. 'I don't want you here,' she said. 'Why did you come back to Leclos?'

'To die,' he said. 'Now, come on. Drink a glass of wine with me. One glass.'

She turned away from him. She fetched two glasses and put them on the table. She closed the anatomy book.

'Corkscrew?' he asked.

She went to her dresser drawer and took it out. It was an old-fashioned thing. She hardly ever drank wine any more, except at Honorine's. Louis put the wine on the table. 'May I take my coat off?' he said.

Under the smart mackintosh, he was wearing comfortable clothes, baggy brown trousers, a black sweater. Mercedes laid the mackintosh and the yellow scarf over the back of a chair. 'You don't look as if you're dying,' she said. 'You've got quite fat.'

He laughed. Mercedes remembered this laugh by her side in her father's little vegetable garden. She had been hoeing onions. Louis had laughed and laughed at something she'd said about the onions.

'I'm being melodramatic,' he said. 'I'm not going to die tomorrow. I mean that my life in Paris is over. I'm in Leclos now till I peg out! I mean that this is all I've got left to do. The rest is finished.'

'Everything finishes,' said Mercedes.

'Well,' said Louis, 'I wouldn't say that. Leclos is just the same, here on its hill. Still the same cobbles and smelly gutters. Still the same view of the sea.'

'You're wrong,' said Mercedes. 'Nothing lasts here in Leclos. Everything folds or moves away.'

'But not the place itself. Or you. And here we both are. Still alive.'

'If you can call it living.'

'Yes, it's living. And you've baked a cake, I see. Baking is being alive. Now, here. Have a sip of wine. Let me drink a toast to *you*.'

She needed the wine to calm her, to get her brain thinking properly again. So she drank. She recognized at once that Louis had brought her expensive wine. She offered him a chair and they both sat down at the table. Under the harsh light, Mercedes could see that Louis' face looked creased and sallow.

'Honorine told me you'd been hiding from me.'

'I don't want you here in Leclos.'

'That saddens me. But perhaps you'll change your mind in time?'

'No. Why should I?'

'Because you'll get used to my being here. I'll become

part of the place, like furniture, or like poor old Vida up at the church with her broken foot.'

'You've been in the church? I've never seen you in there.'

'Of course I've been in. It was partly the church that brought me back. I've been selfish with my money for most of my life, but I thought if I came back to Leclos, I would start a fund to repair that poor old church.'

'The church doesn't need you.'

'Well, it needs someone. You can smell the damp in the stone . . .'

'It needs *me*! I'm the one who's instituted the idea of economy. No one thought of it before. They simply let everything go to waste. *I'm* the one who understood about the candles. It didn't take a philosopher. It's simple once you see it.'

'What's simple?'

'I can't go into it now. Not to you. It's simple and yet not. Simple and yet not. And with you I was never good at explaining things.'

'Try,' said Louis.

'No,' said Mercedes.

They were silent. Mercedes drank her wine. She thought, This is the most beautiful wine I've ever tasted. She wanted to pour herself another glass, but she resisted.

'I'd like you to leave now,' she said.

Louis smiled. Only in his smile and in his laughter did Mercedes recognize the young man whose wife she should have been. 'I've only just arrived, Mercedes, and there's so much we could talk about . . .'

'There's nothing to talk about.'

The smile vanished. 'Show me some kindness,' he said. 'I haven't had the happy life you perhaps imagined. I made a little money, that's all. That's all I have to show. The only future I can contemplate is here, so I was hoping –'

'Don't stay in Leclos. Go somewhere else. Anywhere . . .'

'I heard about the fire.'

'What?'

'The fire at the laundry. But I think it's going to be all right.'

'Of course it's not going to be all right. You don't understand how life is in Leclos any more. You just walk back and walk in, when no one invited you . . .'

'The church "invited" me. But also Madame Picaud. She wrote and asked me what could be done when the laundry burned down. I told her I would try to help.'

'There's no insurance.'

'No.'

'How can you help, then?'

'I told you, all I have left is a little money. One of my investments will be a new laundry.'

Mercedes said nothing. After a while, Louis stood up. 'I'll go now,' he said, 'but three things brought me back, you know. St Vida, the laundry and you. I want your forgiveness. I would like us to be friends.'

'I can't forgive you,' said Mercedes. 'I never will.'

'You may. In time. You may surprise yourself. Remember your name, Mercedes: Mary of the Mercies.'

Mercedes drank the rest of the wine.

She sat very still at her table, raising the glass to her lips and sipping and sipping until it was all gone. She found herself admiring her old sticks of furniture and the shadows in the room that moved as if to music.

She got unsteadily to her feet. She had no idea what time it could be. She heard a dog bark.

She got out her candle moulds and set them in a line. She cut some lengths of wick. Then she put Louis Cabrini's waxen heart into the rounded saucepan and melted it down and turned it back into votive candles.

The Daily Telegraph Cheltenham

Festival of Literature

The Cheltenham Festival of Literature started life in 1949 and is now the oldest and largest annual literary festival in Great Britain. Taking place over a week or two in early October, it offers a varied and full programme of live events celebrating the written and spoken word – talks, discussions, readings, workshops, plays, films. Professional writers of all kinds, as well as others who have caught the imagination of the reading public, talk about their work in a festive atmosphere at the Town Hall and other venues in Cheltenham. Since 1991 the Festival has enjoyed the overall sponsorship of *The Daily Telegraph*.

The Cheltenham Short Story Commission, which was started in 1991, invites leading writers to write a story to be read by them at the Festival. These readings are sponsored by the Friends of the Festival.